D0605663

12/21

OVER, BEAR!
UNDER, WHERE?

Words by Julie Hedlund
Pictures by Michael Slack

PHILOMEL

PHILOMEL BOOKS
An imprint of Penguin Random House LLC, New York

First published in the United States of America by Philomel Books,
an imprint of Penguin Random House LLC, 2021

Text copyright © 2021 by Julie Hedlund
Illustrations copyright © 2021 by Michael Slack

Penguin supports copyright. Copyright fuels creativity, encourages diverse voices, promotes free speech, and
creates a vibrant culture. Thank you for buying an authorized edition of this book and for complying with
copyright laws by not reproducing, scanning, or distributing any part of it in any form without permission. You
are supporting writers and allowing Penguin to continue to publish books for every reader.

Philomel Books is a registered trademark of Penguin Random House LLC.

Visit us online at penguinrandomhouse.com.

LIBRARY OF CONGRESS CATALOGING-IN-PUBLICATION DATA IS AVAILABLE.

Manufactured in China

ISBN 9780593203552

10 9 8 7 6 5 4 3 2 1

Edited by Talia Benamy
Design by Ellice M. Lee
Text set in Gill Sans MT Std

The art is digitally painted using photoshop.

This book is a work of fiction. Any references to historical events, real people, or real places are used fictitiously.
Other names, characters, places, and events are products of the author's imagination, and any resemblance to
actual events or places or persons, living or dead, is entirely coincidental.

The publisher does not have any control over and does not assume any responsibility for author or third-party
websites or their content.

For Jane Yolen—
mentor, friend, and fellow lover of loons
(of the avian variety).
—J. H.

To Iggy and LuLu.
My loyal and lovable companions.
—M. S.

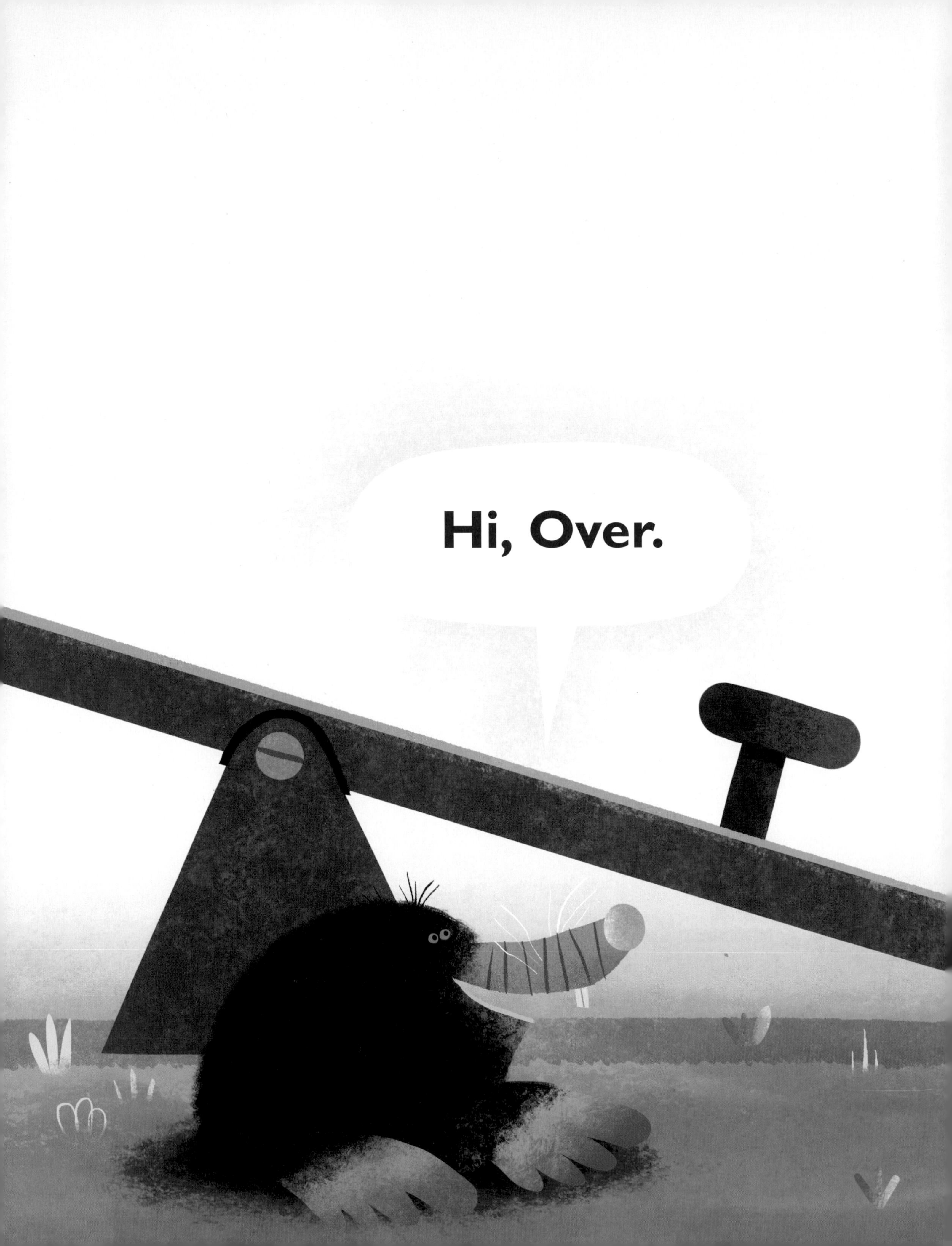
Hi, Over.

Hi, Under.

Over is over Under.

Under is under Over.

Under is over Over.

Over is under Under.

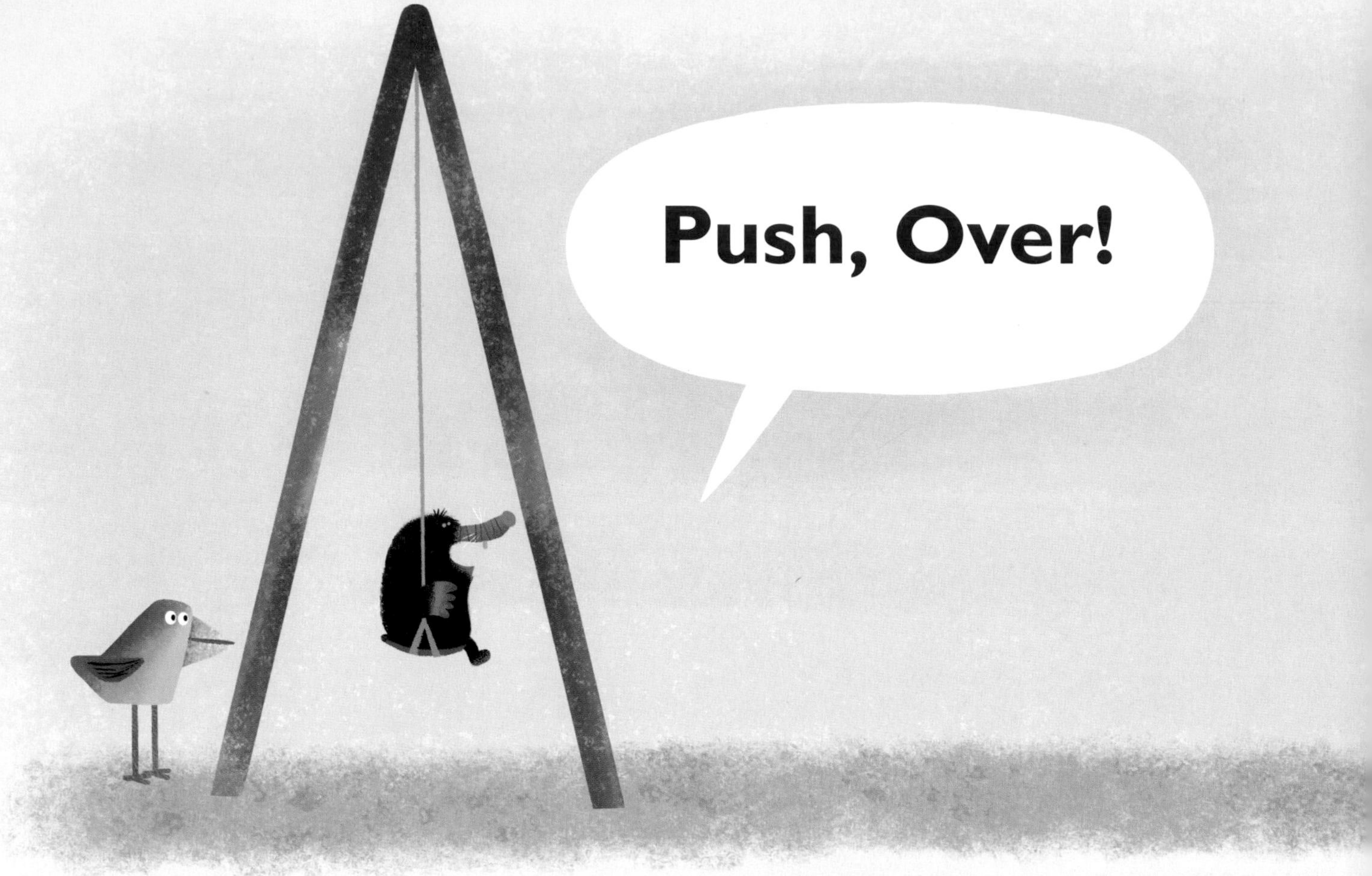
Push, Over!

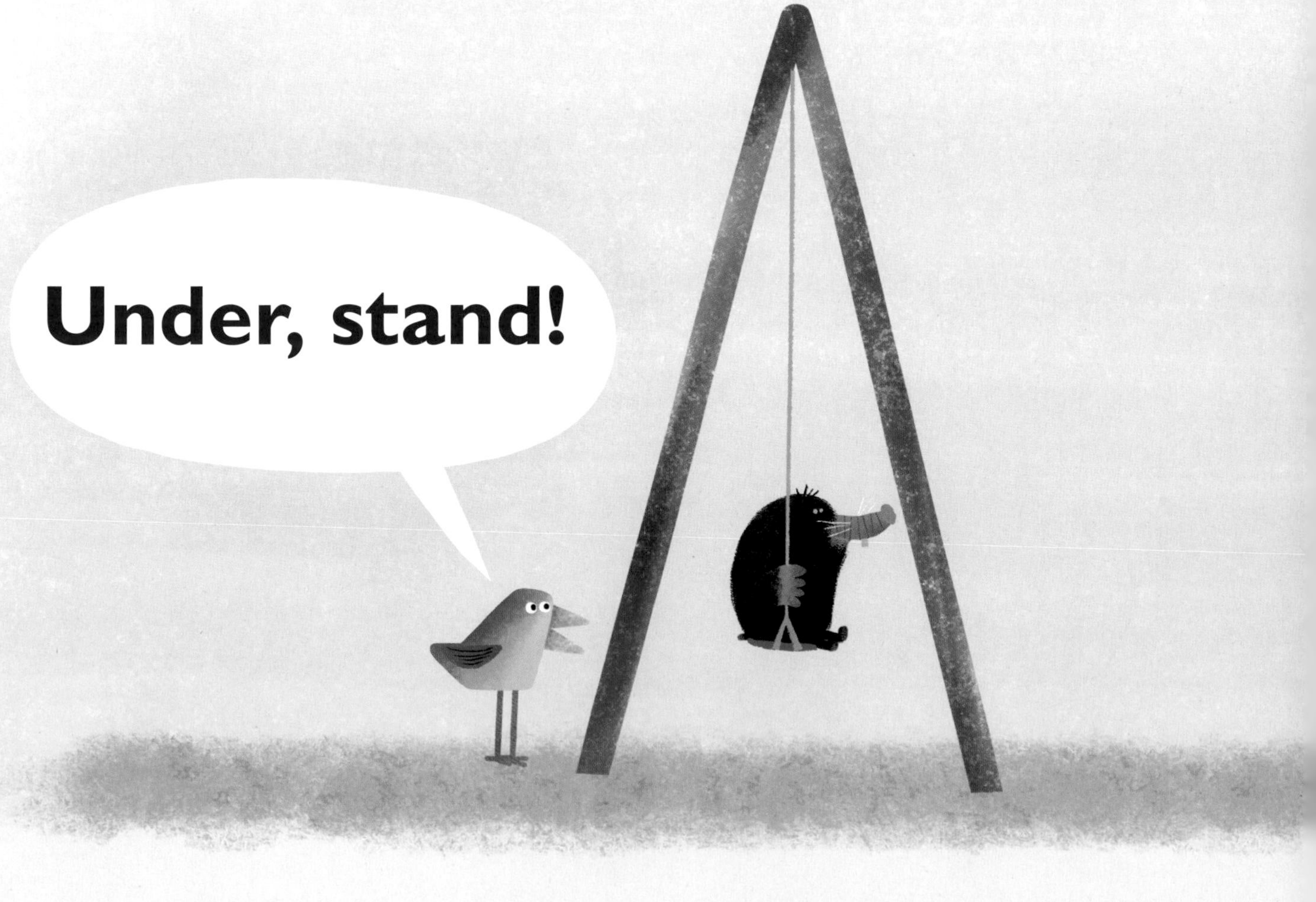
Under, stand!

Under is
over Over.

Over is over
Under.

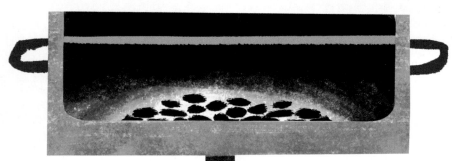

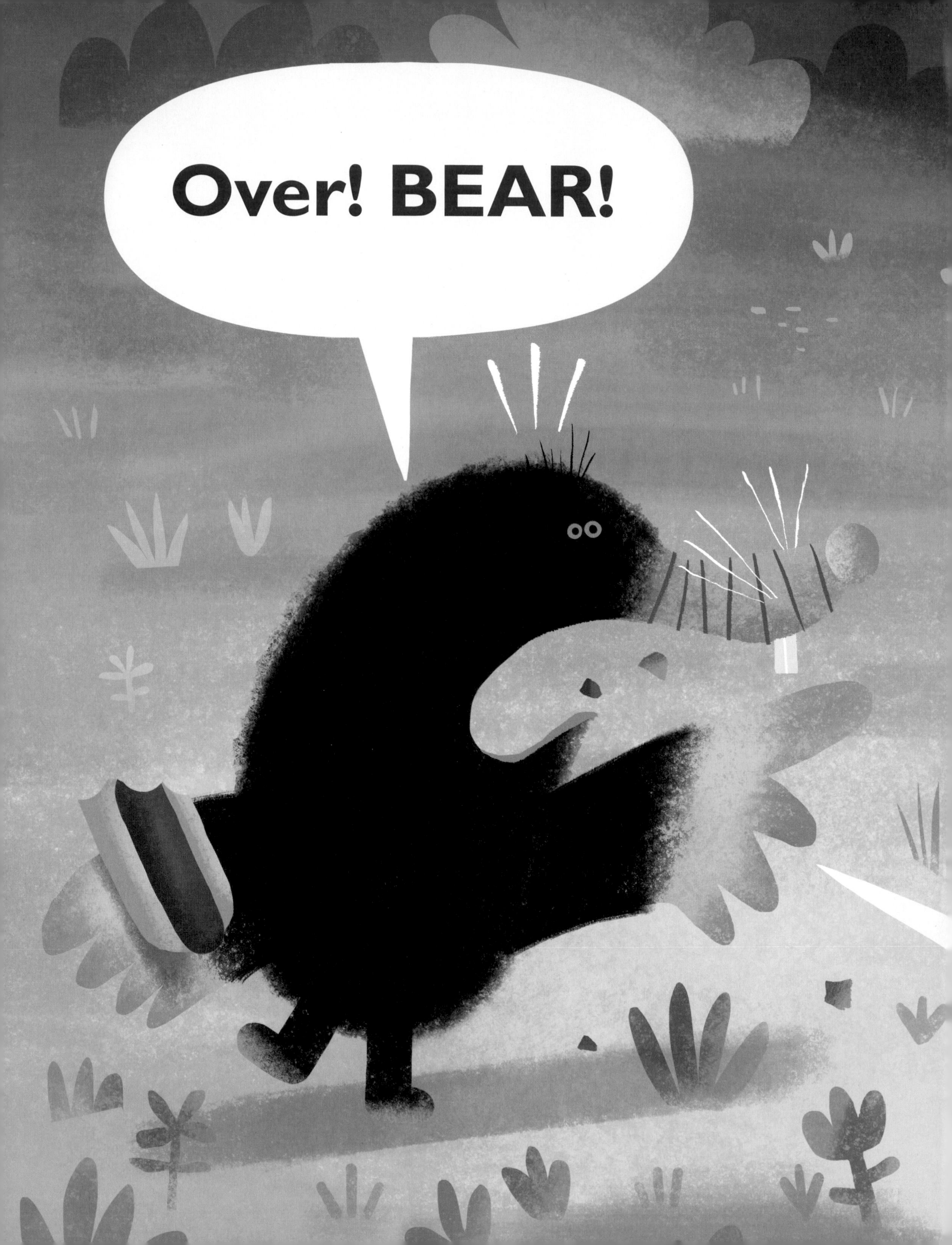
Over! BEAR!

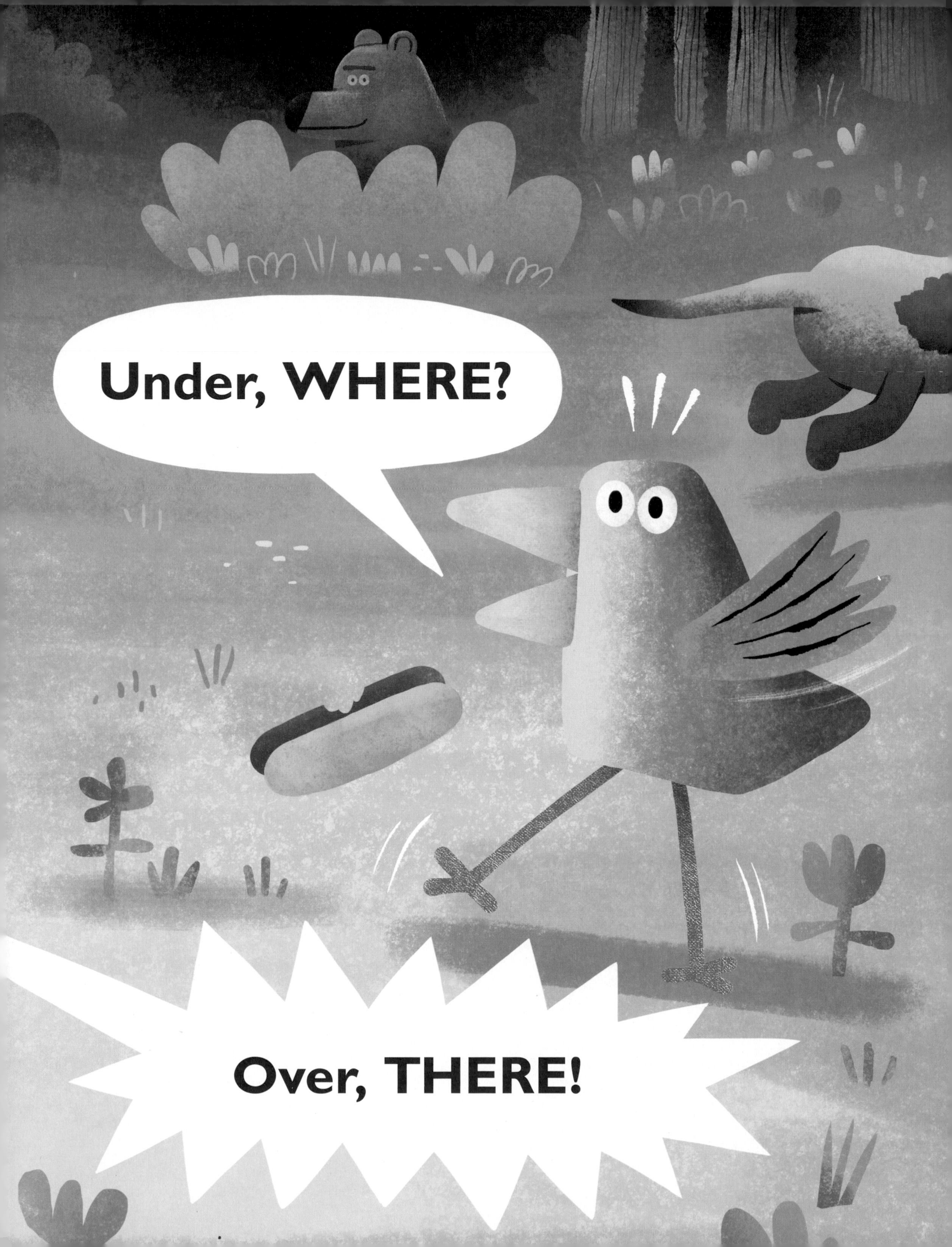
Under, WHERE?
Over, THERE!

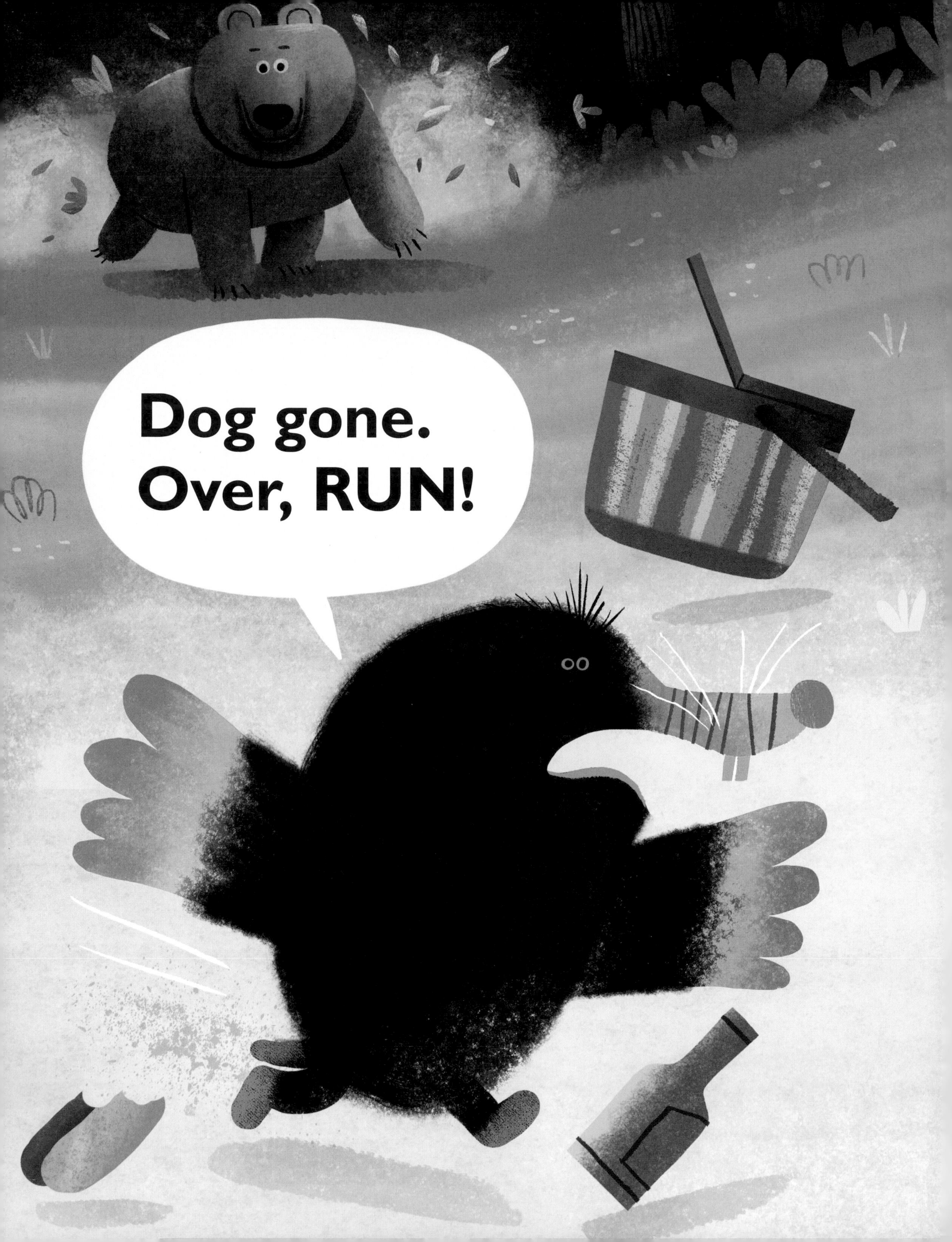
Dog gone. Over, RUN!

Under, GO!

Bear's behind.

Bear's between.

Bear's behind?

Over is over Dog.

Under is over Over.
Sand is over all.

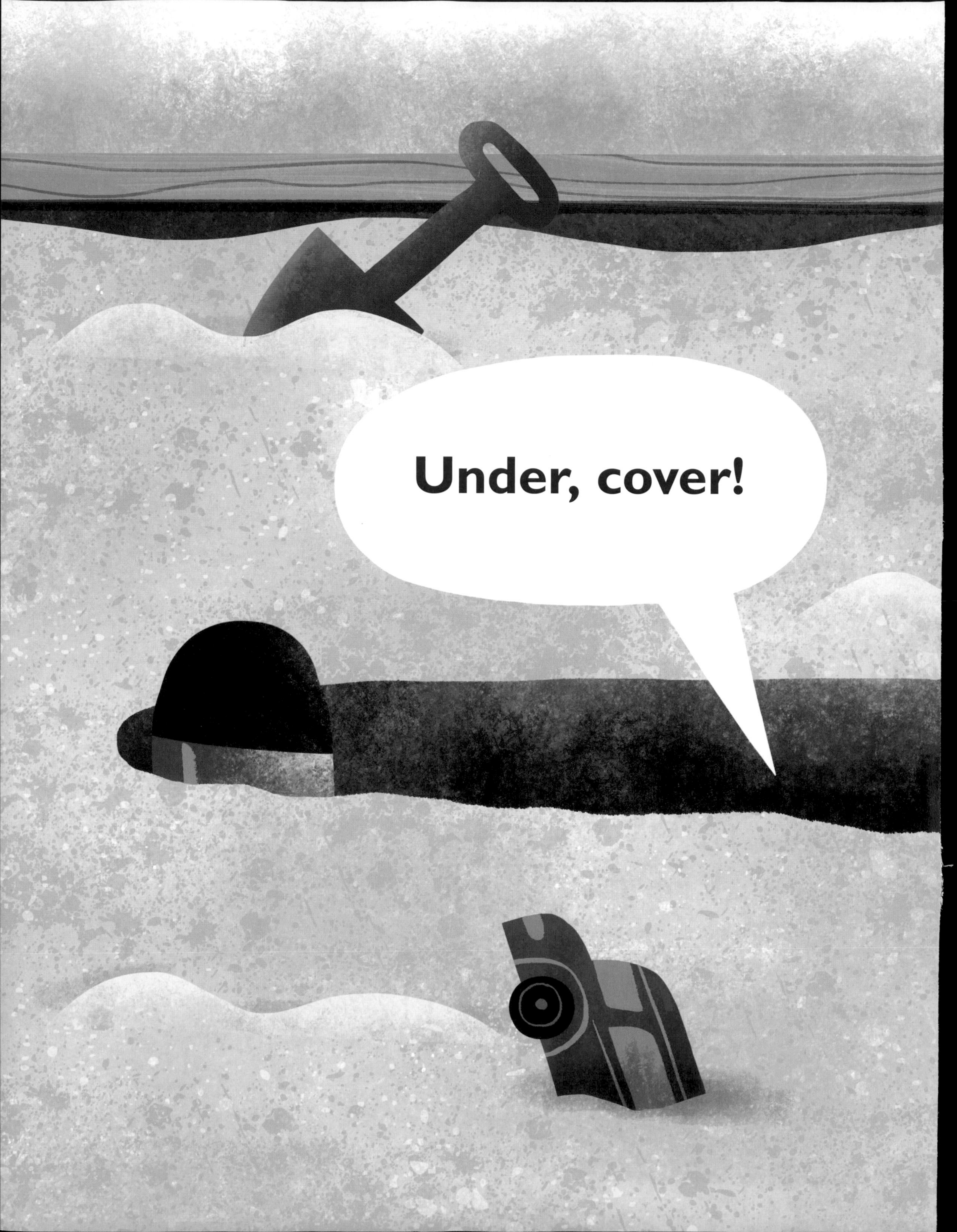
Under, cover!

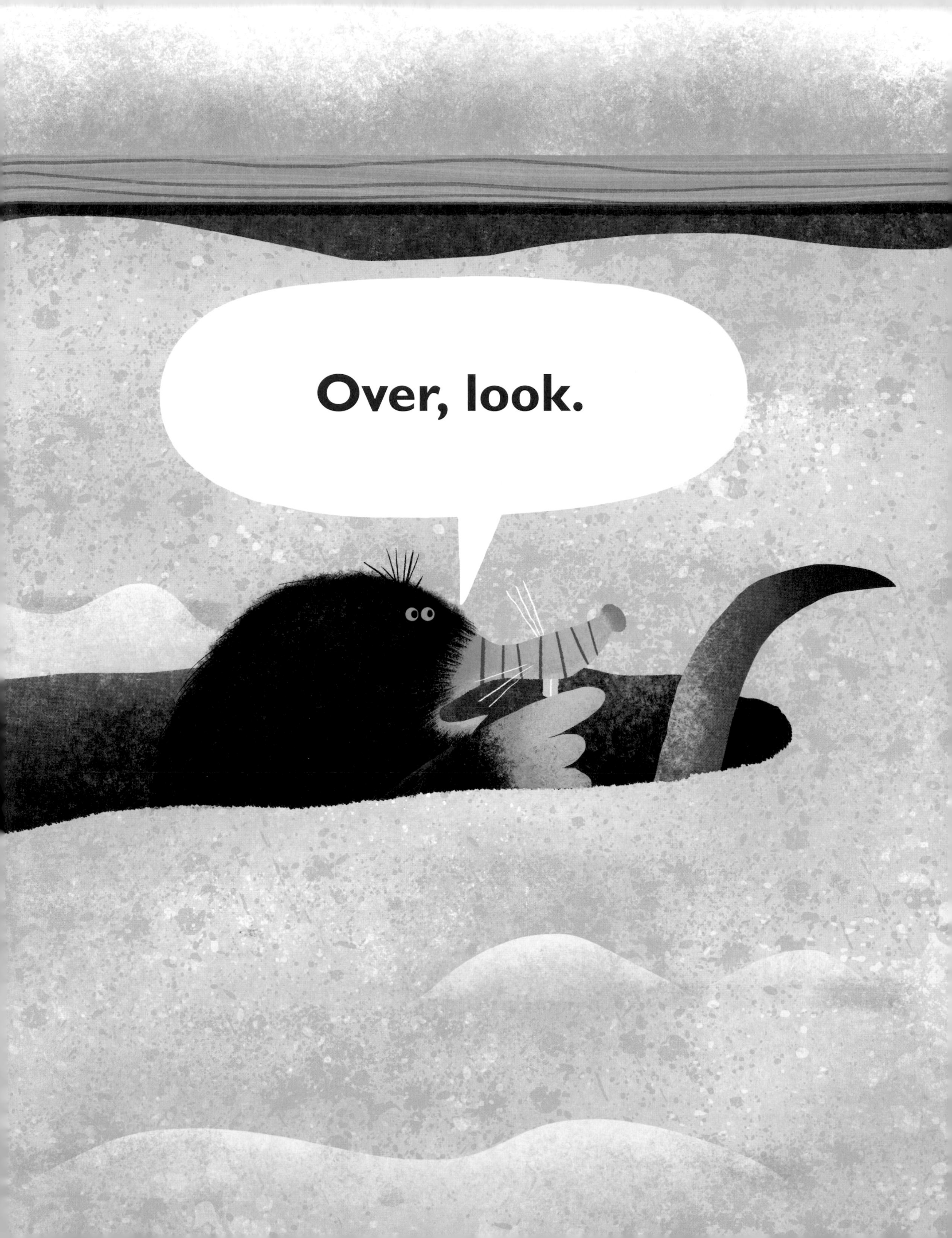
Over, look.

Bear hugs.

Over,
Under,
Dog
are all over Bear.

AUTHOR'S NOTE:

UNDER and OVER are the names of characters in this book, but they are also words that can be combined with other words to create NEW words, which are called compound words. Pretty cool, right?

Can you find words in this book to combine with UNDER or OVER to make new words? How about other words you know that have come together to make totally different words?

FULL LIST OF COMPOUND WORDS TO FIND:

PUSHOVER—A person who is easily made to do what others want them to do.

UNDERSTAND—To know what something means.

OVEREAT—To eat too much.

UNDERCOOK—To not cook something enough.

OVERDONE—To have cooked food too long, or to have done too much at one time.

OVERBEAR—To crush or press down with great force or strength, whether physically or symbolically.

UNDERWEAR—Clothing worn next to the skin and under other clothing. (In this story, you'll see the words "Under, where?"—which is a different spelling but sounds the same. This is called a homophone!)

DOGGONE—A word used to indicate surprise, frustration, or anger.

OVERRUN—To overflow or spread quickly. To go beyond or above an expected place, time, or cost.

UNDERDOG—A person expected to lose a contest or game.

UNDERGO—To go through an experience.

UNDERSIDE—A side that is underneath another; the bottom side.

OVERALL—Something that includes everything as a whole or with all possibilities taken into account.

UNDERCOVER—Being involved in secret work or activities.

OVERLOOK—To look over from a higher place. To ignore or fail to notice someone or something.